THE TEARS OF
RASPUTIN

AL DUNFORD

authorHOUSE®

AuthorHouse™
1663 Liberty Drive
Bloomington, IN 47403
www.authorhouse.com
Phone: 1 (800) 839-8640

Published by AuthorHouse 01/14/2016

ISBN: 978-1-5049-6661-0 (sc)
ISBN: 978-1-5049-6660-3 (e)

Print information available on the last page.

Any people depicted in stock imagery provided by Thinkstock are models, and such images are being used for illustrative purposes only. Certain stock imagery © Thinkstock.

This book is printed on acid-free paper.

CONTENTS

CHAPTER 1

THE LOSS

My grief all lies within, and these external manners of lament are merely shadows
to the unseen grief that swells with silence in the tortured soul.

—William Shakespeare

The highway itself was like an old friend. I had travelled this particular stretch, from Brunswick to the Longfellows, over eight years of road-trips, through every mess of ice and snow that Mother Nature could possibly conjure. The hills could be challenging in winter weather…tedious to climb and tortuous to descend. The card games then, were as much a distraction from the nerve-jangling whiteouts and white-knuckle lurching and skidding, as they were a way to kill time. But on this clear, cool, autumn morning, it was an altogether different kind of dread that I struggled to evade. With effort, every familiar bend in the road, or lakeside vista, could trigger a memory and keep my mind from coming to rest in the present. I focused on the dashboard clock. Less than an hour to Yarmouth. My stomach was not good.

I had watched the military funeral yesterday from the comfort of my living room. I remembered thinking that our country pays tribute to those who serve…the fallen…. as well as it can be done. But to fall in battle is one thing….to fall in the office, in the recruiting centre… at the hands of your colleague….the procession…the 21 gun salute….the flag-draped coffins… thirteen of them…confused emotions…unbearable sadness…but anger and terrible, terrible frustration….desperation for explanation….for some thread of logic or perspective to cling to.

Of course the cameras missed no opportunity to focus on Bud's pain. But it was buried somewhere. Maybe it's buried in the vice-presidential manual somewhere. There is no room for personal grief in statesmanship. The nation comes first. Bud's family, generations of O'Dwyers, had served nobly in every campaign dating back to the War of Independence. That Stephen would continue that tradition and attend West Point was written by this ancestral allegiance pact. Most of those gathering this morning, family and friends, were previously scheduled to attend the send-off for his first tour of duty to Afghanistan, only weeks away. But Dr. Hassan had poked his jihadi nose in the family's business….worse than that…..he'd taken a chainsaw to the illustrious O'Dwyer family tree.

I slowed as I entered the town and passed the welcome sign….Bethesda, Maine, founded 1760. Bud's estate lay just ahead on the left, behind a low, dry-laid, stone wall that meandered through the pines. It was to be a small group…only the immediate family and closest of friends, but the parking had spilled over to the main roadway. I pulled over and parked behind the furthest vehicle. I could use the walk to clear my head and calm my insides. I hadn't seen Bud since our last industry symposium at the Pentagon. It was the anticipated first few words that tormented me these past several hours. What should I say? What could I say? I relaxed a little at the thought that Suds and Mac would be there as well. I imagined we might approach him together, trying to make natural that which was impossibly not. Our best friend has just lost his only son to ….to what?…. a premeditated act of barbarism?...martyrdom in the name of Allah?....an act of pure insanity.... a random, freak, cataclysmic shudder of cosmic circumstance? That speculation was a matter for others; for some other time. For those of us gathered in Bethesda this morning, it was time to close ranks; time to deal with the raw, grinding, impenetrable, soul-numbing grief.

Bud's private security detail were stationed around the property perimeter, and I was submitted to a passport check at the main gate. The O'Dwyer family's right to mourn the passing of their child privately, would be respected to the extent *national* security allowed. I'd always thought the general public, in their cynicism and focus on the ambitions and moral flaws of their elected leaders....Congress...Governors...Presidents...often failed to acknowledge the personal sacrifices that went with public service; perhaps none greater than the right to grieve alone; away from the prying eyes of the masses.

Mac and Suds were waiting for me on the porch. I knew they would be feeling as uncomfortable as I was. In our careers we were familiar with "pressure" situations, of various descriptions, but there was no training for this. No guidebook for how to approach your best friend at the funeral of his only son, gunned down in the prime of his life; his only apparent crime, that of following the family tradition of service to his country. "Boys...how we doin?" I spoke first. "Have you seen Bud yet?" "No. We've only just arrived ourselves," Mac responded. "Suds and I were thinking it would be best if the three of us approached him together." "Ya, we were thinking it would be easier for Bud," Suds offered. The three of us looked at each other knowingly. We all knew it wasn't Bud's discomfort that was our immediate concern.

There were maybe thirty or forty attendees….Bud and Susan's brothers and sisters and their families, Susan's second husband, and a small circle of friends. We joined the comfort line and waited our turn to offer condolences. We took turns trying to deal with *our* discomfort… our awkwardness. We were lifelong friends, separated for months with the demands of careers and families, in homes that were states apart. Two of us were classic 'bull-shitters'; gift of the gab you might say. Mac was the quiet one. Normally we'd be tripping over ourselves with digs and smartass banter, but...well... you know...not now...not here. "It's such fucking bullshit," was all I could offer. Mac and Suds nodded.

We reached Susan and…what's his name…Mark I think...or was it Martin? I put my arms around her. "We're so happy you could be here Alec," she said. "It means so much to Bud. He's going to need all the help he can get." "No choice Susan. Bud has always been there for us," I responded. We had to wait while Bud acknowledged the sympathies of a couple in front of us...a brother-in-law and his wife I thought. We came together as a foursome....no words....back in the high-school huddle....a painfully, emotionally-laden huddle. "Bud, we will be as close as you need us to be...you can count on it. Just let us know and we'll be there," Suds spoke for the three of us." "You fellas were Steve's favourite uncles. He never stopped talking about our last trip to the lodge. A bunch of kids he said. Apparently you guys brought out the teenager in the Vice-President. He loved the idea." At that a white-haired gentleman in an immaculate black suit came up to Bud and indicated it was time for the procession.

The family estate had been passed down through generations. A private graveyard, a few hundred metres through the wood, was the final destination of many bygone O'Dwyers, and it had been readied for its latest inductee. The guests were gently instructed to fall in behind the carriage waiting outside the main door. Six young men, Stephen's closest friends we were told, lifted the casket onto their shoulders and carried it deftly to the one-horse carriage. The group fell in behind Bud, Susan and her husband, and began the final leg of Stephen's pre-empted life journey.

I'd always loved the Maine woods this time of year. It was the silence that cried out. Gone was the ubiquitous buzz, croak, howl, and chatter of nature's summertime tenants. A soft wind blew through the leafless trees without a sound. It was as if the landscape itself gave way... bowing in solemn reverence to the human procession before it. In times of stress, I had developed my own defense regimen. My personal "deep breathing" exercise involved a zooming out from my surroundings. Way out. To where the earth was a mere blue speck against a background of blackness...of the silence of space. To where the universe was clearly paying no heed...not a glance my way. Sometimes it worked...sometimes it just intensified the loneliness. But it wasn't just the silence...the stillness... of this imagined cosmic canvas that offered me therapy. It was universal order juxtaposed on the disorderliness...the messiness of my life...of our lives...where the psychic gold lay.

Speaking of order....the pundits wasted no time connecting the dots of Dr. Hassan's disorderly mind and the chaos created by American neo-cons, (of which Bud was apparently master and facilitator) in Iraq and the Middle East at large. Some even spoke wistfully of the macabre order of Saddam, as being preferable to the arrogant, hubris-induced entropy offered up by we Americans. The "seeds" of democracy had sprouted alright, but mutations were nature's one liners...human nature's last laugh. No doubt, millions of jihadists worldwide, reveled in Bud's personal agony. My reverie was interrupted by the rude caw of a raven. "Hey, aren't you supposed to be in Hilton-head by now?" I thought to myself. Mavericks can be irritating.

We reached the crest of the hill and the path opened to the clearing of the cemetery. The young pallbearers struggled to get the casket in position. Bud's priest took command of the ceremony as the mourners took their positions:

> *"God our father, your power brings us to birth. Your providence guides our lives, and by your command we return to dust. Lord, those who die, still live in your presence. Their lives change but do not end. I pray in hope for family, relatives and friends, and for all the dead known to You alone. In company with Christ, Who died and now lives, may they rejoice in Your kingdom where all our tears are wiped away. Unite us together again in one family, to sing Your praise forever and ever...Amen."*

The prayer ending was the signal for the flag to be removed from the casket and folded...a rehearsed ritual. Susan turned. She held her hand to her face...amidst muffled sobs and the offer of a tissue from Mark..or Martin, she made her way through the onlookers. Bud was motionless before the grave...arms dangling at his sides. And then a lightning bolt from somewhere deep within his pain....he wrested the flag from the shocked official and held it heavenward and thundered. "You cock-sucking, goat-fucking Mohammedans!" The gathering gasped. "Allah akbar my ass," he roared. He pounded the coffin, oblivious to the possible consequences of disturbing the vibrations of the afterlife of his treasured son within. "Wait til you feel *My* God's wrath! ...fuck God...wait til you feel *My* wrath...the wrath of America!" If there were angels in the vicinity, they scattered. I glanced at Father Murphy. He was slack-jawed....apparently years of confessionals, counselling and blessing didn't guarantee much when confronted with the bottomless, visceral, grief that had suddenly found expression in Bud.

Instinctively, Suds and I took a step toward him, but national security reappeared in the form of two agents who had been inconspicuous to that point. Apparently the unravelling of a Vice President was not in the national interest. They got him under control and gently removed the flag, before ushering him through the crowd. Stunned family members looked at each other in disbelief. The maverick raven once again broke the silence. The caw in the distance was nature's exclamation point to a most unnatural turn of events.

CHAPTER 2

ISLAM SLAMMED

I noticed Bill McClelland, Bud's Chief of Staff, in a hushed conversation with who I understood to be the funeral director. The latter stepped before the gathering and announced that the family had decided they needed time alone. We could be confident Bud and Susan knew our thoughts and prayers were with them, but any further efforts of consolation were ill-advised, he suggested. In other words, you should all go home. The crowd began to move when McClelland interrupted. "I'm sure you all appreciate the sensitivity of what you have witnessed today. It would be in the best interests of all of us, as friends of Bud, and out of respect for Bud, in this time of his unbearable sorrow, not to be heard repeating any of what you may have thought you heard here today...thank-you." At that, the throng of mourners dispersed. A sorry sight...a doubly sombre, bewildered, emotionally-jangled, entourage, retraced their steps through the sun-filtered woods, back down to the estate manor.

"I don't know about you guys, but I could use a drink," I offered, exposing my personal shock. "Look, I know you two planned to stay the night, but why not come back to Portland with me? Chances are you won't have any access to Bud anyway. What's the point of hanging around?" "You're probably right," Mac responded. "What do you think Suds? Shouldn't we at least try to get a note to him or something?" "No, we can all message him tomorrow...let's just give this...give him.... some time and space," was Sud's take. "Ok, then you guys gather your stuff and I'll bring the car around and I'll meet you in the lounge. The three of us could use a stiff one for the road," I offered lightly, trying to salvage the mood from the extra leagues it had descended.

The return trip from Bethesda to Portland would take a little more than five hours. We had planned to stop for dinner at about the three hour mark. Thirty minutes in, and hardly a word had been uttered. The three of us had followed distinctively different career paths and worked in very different cultural milieu. We were lost in thought, filtering the day's events through our personal prisms. Milt McConnel was a Middle Eastern Specialist in the State Department. He had been a busy man, much sought after by the talking heads of the news networks, leading up to the Iraq war, and even busier in its aftermath, trying to explain the chaos left in its wake. Suds, Dr. Ben Suddaby, was a doctor of psychiatry, currently employed by the FBI as a profiler of present or potential candidates for home-grown jihadism. No doubt the profile of Dr. Hassan would soon cross his desk, if it hadn't already. Both came from families of accomplished professionals; Milt's parents were both celebrated historians, and Suds' family were secular Jews from Brooklyn; his father was an architect of some renown.

How did I fit into this mix? …..good question. My roots as a farm-boy in Upstate New York, wouldn't have suggested inclusion in such esteemed company. But we were just kids then….thrown together as housemates at Milton Academy a couple of decades ago. You could probably say that Bud and the boys *belonged* there….Bud by virtue of his *establishment* family, Mac and Suds, by virtue of the loftiness of their academic abilities. Me?....well my virtues were of a different sort. I excelled in the physical realm; more specifically the ice rink. I didn't know it at the time, but my teenage years spent tossing fifty pound hay bales onto wagons on the farm, turned out to be training for my position on the team here at Milton, with all the concomitant socio-economic spinoffs, that were of no concern of mine at the time, but seemed to excite my parents to no end.

My mother was an RN at the local hospital. Her income helped to even out the peaks and valleys of the beef markets, allowing my father to pursue his passion for the simple life on the farm. We weren't exactly poor, but there were times. I'll never forget "mad cow Christmas" for example. The new Bauer skates and state of the art carbon sticks didn't materialize that year. My sisters and I were taught to be grateful for what we had. God's bounty was not to be measured in earthly paraphernalia….high-tech hockey equipment in my case. And although I accepted this Christian wisdom at the time, my four years at Milton would change my world view…change *me*…in no insignificant way.

The highway sign read 120 miles to Portland. We agreed we would pull over at the next rest stop. Mac weighed in with what all three of us had no doubt been working through mentally on the trip home. "Jesus, can you imagine the shit that would fly if the media ever got hold of this?" he asked rhetorically. When it came to the relationship with Islam, the state of the union had become "unsettled", to put it mildly, as a result of recent events. The massacre at Fort Hood had been the latest rupture to a build-up of anti-Muslim bigotry since 9/11; since the apparent ingratitude of the natives, in the aftermath of the Iraq liberation….the floodgates had pretty much flown open.

"Don't worry…they won't", Suds responded. "You can be sure you won't be reading about this in the New York Times." "And if you're thinking about national security….don't worry about that either. You don't think there are protocols galore, when leaders of the most powerful nation on earth show signs of coming unglued? I'm guessing the Vice President has the "codes" in his briefcase. Not to be unkind to Bud, but I'm pretty sure you don't get to keep the briefcase when they dress you in the straight-jacket! This is nothing. Bud needs some rest…some time away. This will blow over. Look,… grief is so personal. No two people handle it in exactly the same way. Bud will find *his* way," Suds claimed with clinical reassurance.

With hunger getting the better of us we followed the food signs at the exit. After a couple of back stretches in the parking lot, the three of us made our way inside the roadside restaurant and found a table near the back. As the waitress delivered the ice water to our table, I noticed a couple with a young girl a few tables away. Egyptian probably, I thought to myself. Lately I had been dividing my time between head office in Seattle and travel to the Gulf States. Seeing a woman wearing a hijab in a restaurant was hardly noteworthy for me. "Good evening gentlemen….what can I get for you tonight", our server asked politely. "How are you tonight Madeleine? (her name prominently displayed on her blouse)…..busy place," I added. Since my divorce, I had become boringly flirtatious with any and all, according to Mac and Suds. I hadn't noticed. After orders had been taken, I followed up where we left off in the car. "But the Democrats would have a field day with this would they not?" I asked. "If they cravenly tried to make a case that comments uttered by a man who has just lost his son….even though the man just happens to be the Vice President….is somehow reflective of the foreign policy of the government….well….I think it would surely backfire…I don't think they would try, even if the opportunity was there. Let's just say that funerals of young soldiers are accepted as bi-partisan events," Suds declared.

Our food had been served and we were about to dig in when a too loud….too deliberately loud…voice, from the diner counter intruded. "It's high time we showed these Ar-rabs the door….they come here….they wrap themselves in our flag…they dine at our tables…they take our jobs….they whine about Our Father Who Art in Heaven…they suggest Christmas should really just be "the Holiday Season"….next thing you know they will insist on their own laws." I looked over expecting to see some unshaven, flannel- shirted, redneck lumberjack, just in from the woods….my own prejudice exposed. Instead, three thirty-somethings in business dress were having beers at the counter. Maybe partially alcohol- inspired, the public rant was probably intended to impress the pals, but there could be no doubt who the target of the barbs were. I looked over at the young Muslim family and they were doing their best to appear unperturbed…focused on their dinner.

"They swore allegiance when they came here….they should be forced to renew it every six months….a kind of tentative citizenship….." the loudmouth continued. "Forget that, how about checking into the local police station everyday….we can't afford 24-hour surveillance," his colleague amended the slag. "If we don't nip this in the bud, none of us will be safe. I've had enough of this jihadi shit. Scares the piss out of me." Suds and Mac were looking at me. We had a long history together. We knew each other well. None of us had any time for bullies, but if past experience meant anything, I wasn't likely to react very well.

It seemed all eyes in the restaurant were on the Middle-Eastern looking family as they rose to leave, their half-eaten meals evidence of their discomfort. The father approached the cash to settle his bill as the mother and child continued out the door, avoiding any eye contact with the slugs at the counter. "The manager has suggested that there be no charge for your meals sir. We're sorry we couldn't offer you a more pleasant experience," the woman at the cash register announced. The gesture was graciously acknowledged and as the father followed his family out the door, the lout couldn't resist one last parting slur. "They come here for a free lunch and what do they get?"

"You know you've got quite the mouth on you pal?" I shouted across the room. "I'm sure that little girl really appreciated your opinions. Next time, I think it would be better if you kept them to yourself." "Somebody's got to speak up for this country. You should be thanking me," the grunt retorted. "Ya well how about I thank you not to use my meal in a public place as a pulpit for your ignorance sir." Suds and Mac followed me as I got up and moved towards the Neanderthal. "Alec, forget it…it's not worth it," Mac gently guided me towards the door. "Suds…grab the bill…we'll see you in the car," he added, purposely steering me away from a confrontation.

Back on the highway, as we accelerated to cruising speed, Suds and Mac were looking at me with impish grins on their faces. I knew what they were thinking. We had trod this path many times before in our Milton adventures and beyond. "What?" I pretended not to understand. "Asshole!" I exclaimed to broad chuckles.

CHAPTER 3

JOY TO THE WORLD

"You know mom, I dream of your turkey dressing all year long. I've been counting the days," I exaggerated a little. "Yes, well, if that's all it takes to get you home, we don't have to make it a once a year festivity," my mother responded. "What if I went to the trouble once a week...let's say every Sunday...would you plan your schedule around it?" my mother slyly suggested....challenging my culinary sincerity...calling my bluff.

"Oh... but that I could mama...if only my life would allow it...you know I'd be here," I replied in a weak defense of my lengthy absences from the family. "But we choose our own paths Alec. The Good Lord only shines the light. We didn't raise you to believe you were caught up in life's current...thrashing around for a grip. We control our destinies," my father, the sage, interjected. I had been brought up in the spark and shimmer of my Dad's *salt of the earth*, Baptist, countrified, philosophical exhortations. "Remember....you are no better than anybody else, but you're just as good," was one that stuck; a rural paraphrasing of the equal rights of life and liberty before God; all men are created equal.

In terms of destiny, the truth of it was, I had decided to *follow the money*, at a very early point in my education....wherever it led. If I had not been the math and science nerd that I was, the choice might have been simpler. If I had been a humanities guy, in hindsight, I know I would have felt the tug of Wall Street and the rumoured easy riches waiting at the end of that particular rainbow. Little did I know at the time, that it was precisely my adeptness with the logic and syntax of algebra and algorithms, that was in demand, and that would promise huge paycheques in the investment industry...huge returns for conjurers of mathematical *castles in the air* .... for priests of numbers. Guidance counselling had failed me.

But it was biology and physics that really drew my attention. In my Baptist upbringing, I had been nurtured on the stories of the Old Testament. We Baptists tended towards a literal interpretation of the Holy Book. The physical laws of life and the universe represented new ground for me....solid ground. There were no *miracles* in the laboratory...revelations yes... but revelations of reason, and subject to the rigors of the scientific method. Like many of my generation, the shaky edifice of my young faith, could not withstand the science-induced tremors of skepticism, and eventually the whole monument of religion came tumbling down for me.

Crumbling faith aside, it was not a straight line from my science achievements to the armaments industry. Hardly a visit home would go by, without someone in my family describing so and so's reaction to my ultimate calling. "Alec the weapons peddler?!...you've got to be kidding...he hated guns!" I have to admit, there was no small irony in this. I remember like it was yesterday, my first hunting excursion. I had permission to borrow my father's twenty-two....a couple of friends and I, in the back fields, not entirely sure what we were hunting for. I had the rabbit in my sights....but couldn't pull the trigger. It sounds corny...but the words to a Baptist hymn echoed in my brain.....*all things bright and beautiful...all creatures great and small*....I just couldn't do it. Maybe I had watched too many Disney animations or something...I could imagine the furry, family's gathering in the burrow for the evening... anybody seen Pete?"

So you see, my father's protestations notwithstanding, you could hardly refer to my circumstances as destiny. But while I would never concede that I was being dragged along helplessly by life's capricious currents, I could certainly make the case for some serious bandying about by rough seas. I could point to one incident in my life in particular, where it seemed brother fate had *me* clearly locked in his crosshairs.

"Alec, your father and I have trouble keeping up with your travels, but please tell me you're never in harm's way of these ISIS barbarians," my mother pleaded. Like many Americans with only the most peripheral, casual, interest, in events beyond our border...even town borders... my parents seemed particularly rankled and rattled by the neo-lithic atrocities that regularly appeared on their television screen, courtesy of these seemingly deranged Islamic extremists. Despite my parent's very limited knowledge of Middle Eastern geography ....they knew the terms Judaea and Samaria and the fact that Israel was situated uncomfortably in the middle of the fury....I did my best to allay their fears.

"So far so good Mom. My clients are the Gulf States at the moment. If I should go missing, look for me in Dubai, Bahrain or Kuwait City. That's where I spend most of my time away. If it's any consolation, the greatest danger I face in any of these cities, is the possibility of getting run over by an Arab teenager in his father's Maserati....cruising down city streets at 120 km/ hour, high on too many American spy chase movies."

"But who are these guys?" It was my sister Mary. She and her husband Jake were school teachers. Although not particularly interested or versed in the affairs of the Levant, she did know the geography. Actually, since Iraq, most Americans had at least seen the map. But some would argue that the map was only relevant, in that it was a source of much of the current chaos. That we drew the map...not them....them being the Shias, Sunnis, Christians...Syrians, Kurds, Iraqis, Bedouin...on and on...the native inhabitants...we being the Western colonial powers after WWII....was often cited as at the heart of the crisis.

It was Christmas dinner and I really wasn't relishing a dissertation on the origins of ISIS or helping my family work through just who was fighting who in the Middle Eastern cauldron. To my astonishment and relief I heard Bud's name and looked over my shoulder to see his person in the Washington studio of Meet the Press, a popular weekly political news show. "Hey...there's Bud," I seized the opportunity to change the focus of the conversation. I hadn't seen him publicly since the funeral weeks earlier. The family moved their chairs back from the table in unison, some following me to the living room to listen in. As if on cue, Bud seemed to pick up on our conversation. "Listen," he spoke re-assuredly. "Let me be clear. Our nation is not now, nor have we ever been at war with Islam," he declared in response to an unheard question. "Our concerns at the moment are purely humanitarian. While, we believe that it is in our nation's interest to try not only to contain, but to degrade the ISIS capacity...and we are doing this very successfully I believe,...we will not be directly intervening in this conflict... there will be no American boots on the ground in Syria, in Yemen, or anywhere else in the region. We have learned our lesson in Iraq."

No doubt we were watching a pre-taped interview, and Bud was surely with his family at the moment, in this their first Christmas without their son. My first thought was that he had recovered...back from the brink...back in control....back controlling...spinning the message... this was an art, and he was the master. He looked good. He spoke calmly...almost fatherly. I looked round the room and my family was listening intently. They were hanging on every word. I considered the possibility that they were being "hanged" by every word. The world had become a very complex place. Truth, as presented by even the leaders of the most open, democratic society on earth, had long since been buried...minus the funeral rites. It was no doubt good for business that so few were paying attention. Muslims killing Muslims... financed by oceans of oil...our balance sheets were bloated...our share prices through the roof.

"Let us bow our heads in prayer." We had reconvened around the table...the turkey was about to be served. My father gave the blessing:

Lord of heaven and earth
of all nations and peoples
all faiths and no faith
reveal yourself to those who are poor
reveal yourself to those who are powerless
reveal yourself to ordinary people
in their everyday lives,
that this world
might reflect your love
and your glory.
Amen

CHAPTER 4

THE POWERFUL

Some argued that Bud, not the President, was the most powerful man in the nation, and therefore by extension, the most powerful man in the world. It was a confluence of events, that the Founding Fathers could hardly have anticipated, that made the debate plausible. The 22nd Amendment limited the President to two terms. It was intended to circumscribe the authority of any one individual; to mitigate against the possibility of abuse of the executive office by virtue of getting too comfortable holding the reins of government for too long. It didn't apply to the office of the Vice President.

Leading up to the election of 2008, in the wake of the Iraq debacle, the electorate were only too happy to wave goodbye to the incumbent President. His two terms were up. The verdict of the nation was that we had been duped into a war of choice, by a government that deliberately falsified evidence to create the pretext for pre-emptive war...Saddam and his "weapons of mass destruction". The consensus was that a weak, "cardboard" President, had been manipulated by a small group of ideologues in the Republican Party....the *neo-cons* as they had been labeled. A clear majority of the country couldn't wait to give the whole lot of them the boot....Rumsfeld, Wolfowitz, Perle,....and of course Bud; especially Bud.

Their ideology was not exactly new. It had been kicking around the periphery of Republican thinking for at least a couple of decades. 9/11 had shattered our sense of security, and opened a gaping hole in our defences against extremist reactions to threats to the nation. The neo-cons rushed in...flags waving, trumpets blaring, battle hymns a choralling. The actual ideology was simple...like a religion...it could be summed up very succinctly by the unscholarly as, "you feel like fucking with America?....make my day!"

I can't say I was one of the naysayers at the time. I mean I wasn't entirely comfortable with the *spirit* of the movement, if you can call it that. It seemed too much like the bully in the schoolyard....tougher Americans will be running things from this point forward...and there will be no pussy-footing around...you're either with us or you are in our sights...to paraphrase one of the cardboard President's classic lines. And then there was the dastardly "axis of evil".... just to be clear about who topped the checklist of regimes in our sights. But as usual, for me personally, whenever it came to a contest between moral ambiguity and my paycheque....a tug of war between conscience and cash…..I always seemed to be able to rationalize the *sumo wrestler* anchoring the pay line! No-one could deny that the neocons were good for business. Their militaristic, swashbuckling swagger sent our share prices skyrocketing. Neocons and Raytheon, my company, were a match made in heaven. And just when it seemed the wedding party was over, along came the underwear bomber….and hallelujah….the crowd paused at the exit.

When American Airlines flight 867 vanished from the radar and 270 Americans went to a premature, watery grave in the Atlantic, courtesy of a home-grown, lone wolf, al Qaeda operative, surnamed McTavish, the politics of fear re-engaged. In times of war, Americans have traditionally favoured security over politics. We circle the wagons and turn an "all for one…and one for all" face to the world. So what did this mean to the prospects of the GOP on the eve of the 2008 election? It meant the resurrection of my friend Bud. ….the most powerful man in the …. universe??

Only a couple times before in the history of our nation, has a Vice President served under two different Presidents. It wasn't against the rules. It just didn't happen. Why now? The movers and shakers in the Republican Party read the mood…read the political tea leaves. Even the wackos in the Tea Party liked the idea. They decided that *continuity* was a winner. The lucky winner of the Republican primaries had a new running mate….a new old running mate. But what about the general loathing for Vice-President O'Dwyer…the venomous disgust felt throughout the land, at the mere mention of his name, on both sides of the political divide? Easy; there were enough fall guys, and scapegoats implicated in the disasterous foreign adventures of the past eight years, to fill a football stadium. Bud would be cleaned up…dusted off….re-packaged…re-imaged….and hopefully re-imagined in the minds of Americans.

But what about the aforementioned fears of the Founding Fathers? Bud was already very comfortable in the corridors of power. He knew his way around. Answer?…c'mon…. desperate times require desperate measures….the same cliche dragged out to justify all the other dangerous compromises to our constitution and the laws of the land, made necessary by the war on terror. Compared to detention without charge, surveillance without warrant, drone-facilitated executive kill commands….on and on….the flotsam and jetsam of the war on terror….well….would anyone even notice?

Mac was always sourly poking at me for my love of money. He once said he was sure that if I thought the death of my mother would have implications for the stock market, I would be perusing the index before I remembered to mourn…..the prick. But I must admit, that word of Bud's possible resurrection triggered my accounting reflex before anything else. This was money in the bank….for my company…and for me. A clearer mind might have been returning to the scene of the funeral a few months earlier. We were entering new territory as a nation…. more dangerous territory than anyone could imagine.

CHAPTER 5

A PRIMER ON ISLAM?

When I got home from my Christmas break with the family, I received an email from Mac. He was delivering a lecture to an inter-faith group in Seattle in a couple of weeks time and he queried the possibility of getting together. Our forced reunion at Stephen's funeral had been a reminder to me that I had begun to take my friendship with Mac and Suds for granted. Like all valued relationships, lasting friendships take effort. There were always excuses…followed by apologies. But when weeks turn to months, and months to years…well, you start to question how much you really value your friends. Since the breakup of my family, re-invigorating these friendships had taken on more importance. I know, a little selfish on my part.

"Ya sure Mac….that sounds great," was my reply. "I'm off on an extended tour to the Emirates the following weekend, so the timing is perfect. What's the subject of your talk? Mohammed Misunderstood?! I hope not. I'm a little weary of all things religious these days. Maybe I'll sit in and we can go for drinks afterwards. Send me the details….look forward to catching up in more pleasant circumstances," I emailed back.

Mac was an historian by trade, like his parents. His doctoral thesis was on the subject of the Sunni-Shia relationship in the modern world. Some might think a rather obscure, arcane, focus for an agnostic American, but his parents had been very close friends with the Palestinian-American intellectual Edward Said. Mac had been deeply influenced by dinnertime tales of Mr. Said's childhood in Palestine, and he grew up with a deeply-ingrained fascination with the Arab world in general. His hero was T.E. Lawrence and even as a high-school student, Mac knew every treacherous detail of the divvying up of the Arab world post WW1, which he claimed, set the table for the current chaos in the Middle East.

In a boarding school like Milton, it wasn't healthy to be too different. Mac's Arabism attracted more than a little derision. The seniors jokingly started referring to him as Sheikh Mac…or even McSheikh. But when the ribbing crossed the line to bullying…which it regularly tended to, I played the part of big brother. Despite my lack of status, as a scholarship kid, by virtue of my membership on both the football and the hockey team, I commanded enough respect on campus to offer Mac some immunity. If the abuse was verbal, Mac didn't need any help. He gave much better than he got. But that was the problem. Morons exposed, tended to react physically. That's where I would step in. "Hey..back off...he's my friend. You don't get to mess with *my* roomie."

While the course of my life seemed a refutation of my father's theories of destiny, Mac's life would be exhibit A. I'm quite sure none of his former schoolmates at Milton or Bowdoin, would have been surprised in the least, to find him, years later, on their television screens, warning the American public of the dangers and the foolishness of their government's imminent attempt at regime change in Iraq. Nor would they be surprised to find out that he was right; even down to the details.

The two weeks flew by uneventfully. Just the regular humdrum of vying for market share in weapons bazaar. As usual I was a bit late arriving, and by the time I found parking and slid into a seat at the back of the auditorium, Mac was well into his talk.

"Monotheism would seem to have created genuine opportunity for peace and harmony to mankind. But Islam, almost from its inception, would follow the same pattern as the other two Abrahamic religions, and points of disagreement.... conflicting interpretations of exactly what the One God specifically had in mind, quickly rose to the fore. Not unlike the bitter dispute in Christianity which led to the Reformation, the Sunni-Shia divide in particular, was created over details regarding succession.

I checked my watch. I tried to remember....did Mac say it was an hour lecture followed by a question and answer period, or a two hour lecture plus the interactive? Either way this was bound to be a little tedious for me. I was relieved to find out that the lecture was not to be a primer on Islam, but it seemed Mac's intention was to detail and explain the modern day repercussions of this historical rift in Islam. He had begun with the overthrow of the Shah in Iran, and the rise of the Ayatollahs in the very first self-proclaimed Islamic Republic. He described Saddam's uneasiness regarding this development given the very large Shia majority in Iraq. He connected the dots involving the rise of Hezbollah in the wake of the 1982 Israeli invasion in Lebanon, and continued on to the devastating Iran-Iraq war.

Religion either bored me to tears or disgusted me with its bloody toll. No doubt if you collected all the blood spilt over the millennium, in arguments over this detail or that detail.... between Christians and Muslims, Hindus and Muslims, Catholics and Protestants...and yes, between Shia and Sunna, it would fill several oceans. But Mac's subject was of particular interest to me and really, to my industry at large. In my business you had to be on top of all existing or potential conflicts worldwide. The consensus in the armaments industry presently, was that the Sunni-Shia division held the greatest potential for growth of all international strife. And it was exactly my sales area that stood to benefit the most. The Sunni Gulf states, Qatar, Kuwait, Dubai, Abu Dhabi, Bahrain and Oman, in conjunction with their big brother Saudi Arabia, lived in the perpetual shadow of the threat of the Shia Republic of Iran. The two regional powers, like prize fighters, feigned and jabbed, in the larger Middle Eastern ring; feeling each other out, in constant fear that the other would maneuver into a knockout position. Syria was center ring at the moment; a brawl that was continuing well past midnight.

Mac was wrapping up. "And so it is very difficult to predict how this will end. As Americans, I think we have to acknowledge our mistakes….our contribution to fanning the flames of the current sectarian violence. I believe our President is taking the right tact. Let's keep our powder dry and take advantage of every diplomatic channel open to us to cool the conflict. Thank-you for listening and I'll open the floor to discussion and questions."

We had managed to escape the auditorium just after ten, and had settled in at my favourite downtown eatery. "Nice job Mac…you had a very captive audience. I never thought so many Americans cared about this stuff. It's a long way from most of their paycheques isn't it?" "I would have to defer to you on the last point Alec," Mac responded. "When it comes to body counts and paycheques, don't you guys run the show?" Mac answered testily. "Ok…let's not go there….unless you enjoy hearing my pat answer….we only make em and sell em. The government of the people, for the people….decides who we sell em to," I recited. "Ya, subject to a little persuasion from the Adelsons and Kochs of the people," Mac retorted.

"So how are Jen and the kids," I asked, abruptly changing the subject. "They're great. Josh has just been accepted into Yale. Carrying on the family tradition….he wants to do post-graduate study in American Foreign Relations. Can't think of anything more exciting and more deflating at the same time," Mac declared with a look of disdain. He continued, "You know I think that's why I've never tired of lecturing. This year will mark my thirtieth in the classroom. These kids keep me going. They are immune to cynicism. They firmly believe that they can make a difference….to finally get America's place in the world right. They see their nation flailing away in a current of self-interest internationally, (I was reminded of my father's metaphor) and they believe they will be the ones to bring sanity and stability, back to the picture." "But don't you feel some responsibility as the adult in the room, to curb their enthusiasm Mac?" I replied without thinking. "You really believe that's my job Alec? To tell them they're wasting their time. Their ideas will be no match for money and power. Is that what I should be telling them Alec?" "You know that's not what I meant….a little realism in the mix…that's all I'm saying," I replied defensively.

"What's your take on the deal with Iran Mac?" I tried to redirect the conversation again. "Would you put money on the President getting to the finish line with this?" But Mac was not in the mood to be dissuaded from his pet beef. "Depends how many Congressmen you guys have in your back pocket, I suppose. If you come clean with me on that, maybe I would place a bet. I could use a little top up of my salary. I get a little envious of you *masters of the universe* sometimes…with all your toys….your yachts and lamborghinis," Mac responded a little impetuously. "I was actually hoping you could help me a little on how the other guys are viewing this….the Ayatollah and his inner circle of wack jobs," I replied, maybe a little disingenuously. "You disappoint me sometimes Alec. You've had more conversations with Iranian movers and shakers than I have. You know they're not mad men. You've got a slight edge on most Americans who only get to see the bearded jihadists calling for death to America… America is Satan. You as much as anyone, know intimately the games we've been playing in their backyard for the last one hundred years. I don't have to remind you, we haven't exactly been angels. They've done their accounting. They're not mad or stupid. They need this deal badly. You know that."

We soothed the mood with a couple of after dinner liqueurs and I grabbed the tab. Picking the brain of one of the leading authorities on geopolitics in the Middle East, was easily justified in my Raytheon expense account. I dropped Mac off at his hotel and made my way back to my apartment. Mac was right about one thing. Like ducks on a pond, calm on the surface, but paddling like hell beneath, my bosses would be doing their damndest to protect our interests in the coming nuclear deal with Iran. The difficulty was, it wasn't that easy to get our interests straight. The Middle East in 2015 was a rubik's cube of near insolvable dimensions. Cozying up to Iran had tremendous, potentially positive implications….huge possible benefits to our balance sheet. Older partners in the company often talked nostalgically about the halcyon days of the Shah. We apparently had the lion's share of the billions of dollars in weapons trade with Iran then. On the other hand, our Gulf State accounts were making noise about their discomfort with any deal. They viewed American overtures to Iran as a sellout by an ally, and were threatening to secure their arms from more trustworthy and loyal sources. Even Solomon would be scratching his head with this one, I thought to myself. But we were fretting needlessly. Mac, the historian would not be surprised to learn why. The outcome would not be determined by the balance of interests of the military-industrial complex…but rather the balance of one man's mind. Well behind the scenes, a tragedy of Shakespearean proportions was unfolding….a King gone mad with grief, was sobbing off stage…his tears of vengeance were destined to shake the nation to it s core.

CHAPTER 6

INTO THE OVEN

The travel prayer came over the PA as we prepared for takeoff. Etihad was always the carrier of choice for me. I was comfortable with the "whiff" of Islam on these flights. To a non-believer, the Arabic prayer calls could still be remarkably relaxing and soothing. "*Oh Allah you are the facilitator of the journey and the helper in the affair. You are the companion in the journey and the successor in charge of my family, property and son.*" I guess my daughters, had they been travelling with me, were on their own, in Mohammed's way of thinking…or more accurately…in Mohammed's day. Of course I had my faith placed squarely with the designers and maintenance guys of the AirBus 3000 and therefore was impervious to the solace this particular Muslim prayer offered.

As we awaited clearance, I amused myself with ruminations regarding *modern* Islam. It occurred to me, that the ignoramuses who insisted Islam was inherently rigid and violent and as such, a grave threat to Western civilization, had never flown on Etihad. As I sipped my glass of merlot, courtesy of a lovely, Filipino attendant, clad in a stylish purple uniform, I thought of how the Emirates, the Gulf States, were such a refutation of that idiocy. When reminded that there was no shortage of blood and guts and calls for genocide of the unbelievers, in the Old Testament, defenders of the Christian faith would point to the capacity of their faith for *evolution* over time. Islam has no such capacity…it is self-evident…really?…ever been to Dubai? In comparison with the centuries of enlightenment that Christianity has benefited from, the pace of evolution of Islam in the Emirates could only be described as breathtaking. I stared at my glass. The wine inside it was "haram"…a sin against God…it says so in the book…and the book is never wrong. But, like the claims of forward looking and thinking Christians of today, not wrong necessarily…just open to interpretation. The devil is in the details misconstrued or misappropriated. The Divine is in the spirit…in the overall message of love and compassion. According to Mac, this is no less true for the Quran than it is for the Bible. I trusted that he would know.

New York to Dubai was a ten hour flight. I managed to get a little work done between meals and was relaxing over coffee and the news of the day. As previously noted, I had an inescapable habit of filtering news through the lens of the stock market…or more specifically *our* share prices. There were several front page stories that caught my attention. The President had just wrapped up a summit involving the Gulf States and Saudi Arabia at Camp David. His intention had been to assuage their concerns about the impending nuclear deal with Iran. According to the article, he had been less than successful. *"Saudi Arabia is so angry at the emerging nuclear agreement between Iran and the major powers that it is threatening to develop its own nuclear capability – one more indication of the deep differences between the United States and the Persian Gulf Arab states over the deal, which the major powers and Iran aim to complete by June 30,"* the article read. No doubt my ear would be bent by some of these concerns on my current trip, but I was a sales and support guy…not a politico. This was outside my purview, and I was sure as well, that the market would ignore it as bluster. One of the attractions of our industry to investors, is that it was so difficult for clients to change course midstream. Leaving aside the uncontested superiority of our weapons globally, there were issues of training and spare parts. It really wasn't as easy as the Sheikh waking up one morning and deciding he'd rather go Chinese or Russian!

The next story made me smile. Surely I wasn't the only reader who was floored by the irony of the newsline…."*Dark and dangerous times…GOP 2016 hopefuls focus on Islam at Iowa Summit.*" The clowns were jostling for position in the fear-mongering and Israel suck-up line. "*Let me be clear…Iran enemy…Israel friend.* Another, "*an electromagnetic pulse over the state of Iowa would knock us back to the stone age."* And finally, "M*uslim doctors, engineers and scientists could prove very problematic if they embrace this jihadist doctrine of sharia… we are a bunch of crybabies led by stupid people and we can't go on like this!"* Really?....and just how are we to go on?...another pre-emptive strike?....outlaw Islam altogether?....dark and dangerous stone-age indeed!

Yet there was a much more foreboding storyline below…one with very serious potential repercussions in the arms industry long-term. It was Jerusalem Day in Israel. Bibi Netanyahu, fresh from assembling the most extreme right-wing government in the history of the state, was drawing a line in the sands of Arabia…in the sands of time even. His declaration?... *Jerusalem has always been the capital of the Jews alone.* Oh oh….this was tough talk. To even the casual observer, the un-invested, it certainly seemed that the Judaic lemmings were marching headlong towards the cliff. At the moment, our arm sales in the Middle East, were subject to review by the Israelis…yes seriously. It was part of our commitment to assuring Israeli military supremacy in the region. But there were rumblings in the distance…the sounds of American Jews and non-Jews, on university campuses all across the nation, questioning the legitimacy of a democratic state that perpetually held several million of its citizens in apartheid conditions. The BDS…boycott, divestment and sanctions campaign, was a gathering storm, gaining strength from those very same young idealists that Mac referred to as giving him energy and providing hope for the future. To add to the bad omens for Israel, the Holy Father, Pope Francis, had just declared Mahmoud Abbas, head of the Palestinian Authority, an angel of peace, as he went on record as recognizing the State of Palestine.

The seat belt sign came on. I looked out the window at the first hint of Dubai…the jewel of the desert, in the distance. Burj Khalifa, the tallest free-standing structure in the world poked through the clouds. Surely, I thought to myself, as it glittered in the morning sunshine….a monument to the notion that Islam and modernity was not a contradiction in terms.

CHAPTER 7

ON THE ROAD TO THE MODERN WORLD

A quick connection in Dubai and I was on my way to my morning appointment in Kuwait. Lieutenant Colonel Khalili was my contact, and the purpose of my visit was simply to go through the coming year's procurement checklist. I knew he would be peppering me with questions; technical details regarding the actual deployment of many of the weapons on the list. Although I had always been a little skeptical of his Honours Physics degree from the American University of Kuwait (that he managed to slip into every conversation in the past) he consistently impressed me with his grasp of the more complex details of whatever munitions were under discussion. We had become good friends over the past five years of doing business. Much of what I knew about Kuwait and the Arab world in general, I learned from Mustapha Khalili. His driver would be waiting for me on arrival.

A fog of dust muted the morning sun, as we crawled along the ring road in morning traffic. Kuwait was not Dubai. *Things* didn't work as well here. According to Mustapha, hopeless traffic congestion was just one symptom of the parliamentary paralysis that Kuwaitis blamed for their sluggishness on the road to progress. Whereas Dubai, under the benevolent autocracy of Emir Maktoum, had chosen a mad dash to the future, Kuwait's Emir Sabah, a monarch constrained by at least the appearance of democracy, was compelled to take a more circumspect route. Money was clearly not the difference, as Kuwait was awash in petro dollars. It was a common topic of discussion over beers in the Embassy whether religion was a factor. I always taunted my Christian colleagues when they expressed surprise that the same holy book could produce the archaic, conservative Wahabbist outlook of the Saudis and the western-welcoming, fun-loving Islamism of the Dubai-ins. Surely the Bible and the Torah were no less elastic in interpretation. Kuwait was like the Islamic *half-way house*. Mustapha would explain that Kuwaitis were no less *fun-loving*, or less enamored with all things western, than other Gulf Arabs. They were just forced to be a little more discreet about it.

I once challenged him when that discretion seemed to have gone missing in the opulent shopping malls I frequented in Kuwait. I wasn't complaining, but the plunging necklines, short skirts and tight jeans were more prevalent and dare I say, more provocative, than anything you might see in the West…maybe even than in Dubai. "Oh those are not Kuwaiti girls!" he responded. "They're Lebanese or Egyptian or Syrian. Kuwaiti parents would never let their daughters out of the house dressed like that." Although, I'd never witnessed it myself, I was reminded of stories told by embassy colleagues, of flights to Dubai or some other playground in the Middle East, where Kuwaiti women, after boarding in abayas and maybe even veils, would undergo an amazing fashion metamorphosis, and emerge from the plane washroom in much more comfortable….read revealing….western garb! Although, when I considered that veiled women in black abayas were equally represented in the malls, it suggested that maybe Mustapha's observation was accurate. Generalizations by outsiders, involving a culture in flux, were as difficult as the changes themselves were to the participants.

We pulled up in front of the Starbucks and John, the Indian driver, indicated that *Baba*… Colonel Mustapha, had already arrived and was waiting for me inside. As per Arabic custom, we would relax and talk family and news, before moving on to the Defence Department later in the morning, where we would get down to the business at hand. "A salamu aleikum habibi," Mustapha rose and took my hand. The compulsory *double cheek* greeting was something I could never quite get comfortable with. He looked as immaculate as ever in his crisp, white, flowing, angle-length dishdasha. "It is wonderful to see you again. How are things at the center of the world?" Mustapha smiled. "How is your family?" "The girls are great…at least they were the last time I saw them," I replied. Mustapha was well aware, if a little bewildered, at the fragility and fractured state of the Western concept of family. Family connections were as important and powerful as ever in the evolving, modernizing Arab world. "How about your girls? Have they decided where they will study? Let me know if I can help. You know I have friends in high places," I said with a sly grin. "Yes, I recall that offer previously and I have filed it away for safe keeping," Mustapha joked. "But their mother is commandeering their education, although I'm sure I'll be one of the first to know, when that decision is made," he laughed.

We ordered our frappuccinos and continued our greeting ritual. I gathered the newsprint on the table to make space for our trays. "I see you're still getting your news from questionable sources," I joked as I noticed the pages I was collecting were from the Guardian. "Yes well, we have had a rather long relationship with the British, and for the most part it has been a very honorable one," Mustapha responded in an equally playful spirit. Kuwait's history had been as a British protectorate and as a result, Kuwaitis didn't share the burden of a colonial past, which plagued many other nations trying to find a foothold in the modern world. I noticed one of the headlines…..*How many slave deaths for the Qatar World Cup can FIFA put up with?* "Mustapha…did you read this? What in God's name is the lady on about?" I asked. "Oh yes…very interesting," the Colonel responded. "She makes an excellent argument," he continued. "Some would say a bit over the top…a bit sensationalist….but when you're talking about sacrificing lives for football games…well…a little sensationalism might be called for don't you agree?" "I'm sorry I'm not following," I replied bemusedly.

"Qatar's need for, and relationship with foreign workers is no different than ours. The writer has done her homework. I suspect she has her facts straight. She is attempting to put the world spotlight on the appalling labor abuses that take place in Qatar, but she could be talking about any of the Gulf States, including my country. Without a doubt there are cases that deserve the description of *modern day slavery,* which is where the caption comes from. She has done a calculation of construction deaths on World Cup venues, presumably avoidable deaths with reasonable safety guidelines in place, and has come up with this headline grabbing *62 deaths per game* conclusion." "That's got to be a little embarrassing," I said in deliberate understatement. "Let's hope so," was Mustapha's surprising response. "When I first heard that Qatar had won the bid, it was my first thought. The world would be focused on the games, but their society, our societies, would not avoid the reflective glare of the sporting event itself, not unlike Beijing in 2008. This kind of global engagement is the fastest track to change," Mustapha argued. "But is there not a danger that your societies will view this as an endorsement by the outside world, of the status quo?" I responded. "Not as long as there are journalists like this nice lady," Mustapha replied. "I suspect, this is just the first of many critiques of our society that the Qataris surely knew they were inviting, when they bid on this sporting world extravaganza."

Rarely had one of my business trips gone by, without reading about a Filipino maid jumping out the window of a high building, or throwing herself in front of a car on the expressway. As well as ending the misery of enslavement to the family she nannied for, the latter had the surplus potential of securing *blood money,* from the unlucky sod behind the wheel, to help support her bereaved family back in the Phillipines. "Surely Mustapha, your opinion must be a minority one in Kuwait, or you would join the modern world in its revulsion to this…you would crack down on it…no?" I suggested. Mustapha paused before answering. He looked a little frustrated at the question. "Look….I can guarantee you that the maids and drivers of the Al Sabahs, (referencing the Royal Family) are treated as well as any that you would compare with in your country…probably better…they would be considered part of the family here. This would be true of many, many Kuwaiti families, my own included. These are families that have been having tea with the British for going on two hundred years now. We did business, we socialized, we learned their customs…you would arrogantly say we were being civilized….no?" He didn't wait for my answer. "But we are not a homogeneous society, any more than yours is. Our Bedouin families have no such history. They have had in many cases, less than a couple of generations of exposure to Western norms and values. I don't have to detail the tensions. Use your imagination. Check our labor laws….all of this nonsense… this inhuman treatment of Asian migrants is illegal. I also don't have to explain politics to you….surely. When it comes to enforcement, it gets political. Monarchies are delicate things in 2015. If you're not careful, the *breezes* of change can become mighty gales in the blink of a camel's eye," Mustapha responded with typical Arabic poetic flair.

"Listen…Alec…there is so much more I would like to say to you on this. Let me make a suggestion. How about we go get our work done this afternoon, and you join us for dinner tonight. I am hosting a diwaniya this evening, and it would be a great opportunity for you to meet some very interesting people." The *diwaniya* was the Arabic equivalent of men shooting the breeze over coffee at McDonalds back home, only much more formalized and more impactful to the life of the society. Traditionally they served as populist sub-committees to the more influential and powerful *parliament* of the ruling class; a forum for the ventilation of ideas….a chance to vent, followed by a feast!

CHAPTER 8

A CLASH OF CIVILIZATIONS?

Kuwaiti extended families tended to congregate in different areas of the city. Daiya was also home to many of Mustapha's cousins. The Arabesque, multi-story villas were impressive. It was often the case that they would house several families…parents, brothers…close family. John, pulled the car up to the entrance and let me out. I pressed the intercom button at the gate and a young woman answered….probably Ethiopian I thought from the accent. A couple of minutes later, Hala, Mustapha's sixteen-year old daughter, came out to greet me.

"How are you sir," she spoke in unaccented English. How was your trip?" "I'm fine Hala. (It was my job to memorize family names!) Have I convinced you that UCLA is a much better bet than the University of Kent?" I joked. "Ha ha….I have been studying the travel brochures as well as the prospectus. That is an unfair comparison Mr. Alec. I'm afraid my mother is insisting the decision is not based on weather alone," she replied with a teenage giggle. "Please come inside. My father wants to have tea with you before the diwaniya."

Guests to Arab homes are usually entertained in a kind of transitional sitting area. Living spaces are very private. Despite this, I found myself ushered into the TV room in the heart of the home. Rania, the eighteen year-old, rose from the sofa to greet me. I could see she had been watching an episode of Mad Men as I came in. Mustapha and his wife Dalia came into the room at the same time and welcomed me. As part of my training I had been thoroughly versed and rehearsed in the protocols of Arab culture. As usual though, when confronted with modern realities… a culture in flux…much of it was of little value. I didn't hesitate to shake Dalia's hand. You simply had to be awake to which particular Arab world you found yourself in. The Khalilis would be comfortable anywhere in the world…New York, London, Paris… in fact they probably owned apartments in all of those cities.

"I hope you had a good rest in your hotel Alec," Mustapha said. "I have let my friends know we have a special guest tonight, and you could be in for some serious grilling," the colonel chided me. "Yes, well as long as we don't venture into the domain of national security, I'm ready to defend my country," I responded with a smile. "At the risk of exposing my cowardly side though, I need to make it clear I only voted Republican with my pocketbook. I am actually a Democrat in my heart," I added, somewhat disingenuously. "I can't defend every idiotic statement that comes out of the mouths of babbling fools." I was thinking back to the recent Israel lovefest of the 2016 Republican contenders.

"Don't worry Alec. No doubt my friends will be making a very similar point tonight. They will concede that although there is only one American Foreign policy, they know there are many dissenting voices. But they will probably demand a reciprocation….an acknowledgement that although there is only one Islam, there are many flavours. I shouldn't be anticipating the conversation, but I doubt if they will be much interested in Ms Kardashian's latest exploits, for example! It is bound to be slightly more substantive than that," Mustapha warned.

Diwaniya is the term, not just for the social gathering, but for the room itself. Comfortable couches lined the perimeter, and maybe fifteen or twenty men in brown dishdashas were relaxing in quiet but not subdued conversation. As we entered the participants rose to greet us. Colonel Khalili took me round the room, introducing me to each of the men before we took our seats. Mustapha had told me that, although many of the guests were fluent English speakers, the conversation would largely be conducted in Arabic. "Welcome sir," an elderly gentleman greeted me in flawless English. "We are so happy you were able to join us tonight. We trust you brought the latest cutting-edge American weapons technology with you on your visit. It helps me to sleep at night knowing that we Kuwaitis are up to date," he offered with a playful grin. "I promise you I've done my best sir… within the limits of government policy. You must appreciate we like to keep the very latest in reserve. It helps *our* sleep," I replied to laughter.

"Welcome habibi," a greying, headscarfed, paticipant offered. "Alec, let me introduce you to Mohammed Khattib. His son is studying at Columbia presently." Mustapha added. "How are you sir?" I asked. "How is your son finding the weather in New York? It can be a little cool this time of year." "Actually, he's very comfortable there. He has gotten quite active in the Society for Islam on campus. He's encouraged by the opportunities it provides to help explain Islam to his schoolmates. Despite all the bad press lately….ISIL…Charlie Hebdo, and the recent murders in Texas, he claims his peers are very open-minded and receptive. He was telling me about the BDS (Boycott Divestment and Sanctions) vote that was held just recently. Apparently it got very emotional, and caused a lot of bad blood….security was called in a couple of cases where things got out of hand. It is an eye-opener for Arabs to find out that not all Americans are as enamored with Israel as your Governments seem to be. Forgive us, but we get a little weary of the swooning," he commented with exasperation in his voice.

Tea and dates were offered by formally uniformed Asian attendants, as the gathering seemed to move into another phase. The conversation became more centralized…the discussion was taking place across the room rather than with the immediate neighbor. Mustapha translated for me. "That is Mubarak Osman, a Shia colleague of mine. He is not happy about his friend's loss of appeal today. He will have to serve out the full two years he was sentenced to." "What was his crime?" I asked innocently. "He was found guilty of insulting the Emir. You would be surprised how open our press is here….but there are two subjects that are beyond criticism…. the Prophet and the Emir. It's codified in our laws." Mohammed explained. "Both are out of bounds, even for members of Parliament as his friend is."

"Good evening Sir….welcome to Kuwait. We thank-you for joining us tonight," announced a rotund, senior-statesman- looking gentlemen in British-accented English. "Oh oh…get ready for a lecture," Mustapha whispered. "I'm sure Mustapha has shared this with you, but as Muslims, we get so frustrated at things we hear out of America these days and we get no opportunity for clarification. For example….who is this Lindsey Graham guy?" "Uh…I hesitated….if it's the one I think you're referring to…he is a GOP candidate for the presidency in 2016," I answered. I knew where this was going. A week earlier he was quoted at a Jewish fund-raiser as saying that in the Middle East, everything that started with 'al' was bad news. "But how could that be?" the Sheik asked incredulously. Mustapha had scratched me a note… Sheik Ibrahim al Ghanim, Phd in Theology, Oxford. Wonderful, I thought to myself. "Are there no minimum educational requirements for American leaders? Do you not have to have a modicum of knowledge of the outside world, to qualify for the highest office in the land? Could it really be that Mr. Graham is unaware that 'al' is the word for 'the' in our language?" he asked rhetorically. "I don't think that is a plausible explanation. And so I can only conclude that the man is casually, but deliberately, offering insult to the entire Arab world!" He wasn't finished. "And then today I read that the reason he is running for office is….wait for this…. *the world is falling apart*!" "Just what sort of magic glue does he believe he comes bearing?" the good doctor's voice was rising.

"Dr. al Ghanim, with all due respect, it is an election campaign. I fear it won't be the last outlandish statement that comes out of Mr. Graham's or any of the other loudmouths on the campaign trail. I don't think it is reflective of the intelligence of Americans in general. It's all about attracting attention in politics….even if you are attracting attention to your own stupidity, it appears." I replied lamely. "Can I ask you a question sir. How do you feel about the impending nuclear deal with Iran?" I realized it might seem like a rather transparent attempt to redirect the conversation, but I asked this question of Arabs at every opportunity. Kuwait was a Sunni country with a Shia minority. They had a delicate relationship with the Persian power, just tens of kilometres, across the Arabian Gulf to the east, not the least because of the potentially restless minority of the Shiites within. In fact the jailed Ahmed Talabi, previously spoken of, was this community's major spokesperson.

"Of course I don't speak for our nation, but if you are asking my personal opinion, I believe it is the most hopeful, wisest policy development that has emerged from your country in many decades," the Doctor responded. "I'm sorry if I offend you, but it seems you have been rather slow learners when it comes to this grand *war on terror*. The lesson is, you can't annihilate extremism….you can't club it out of existence….you have to *deflate* it. And how you do that is rather straight forward in my humble opinion. It's not quick, but it can be relatively bloodless. You simply start subtracting the grievances. We Arabs are a proud people Mr. Alec. The grievances are genuine. I won't take you through the entire litany. I understand that dinner is about to be served. But let me mention just one. The one that tops the list for all Arabs in every poll ever taken. Every, poor, illiterate, Arab, Egyptian or Persian feels this pain acutely, I can assure you. And that is the pain of the Palestinian farmer who lost his land and his history, to make way for a Jewish state, out of the collective guilt of the world as a result of the Holocaust. What makes this narrative so powerful is its simplicity and the totally abject affront to fairness and justice that doesn't take a scholar to acknowledge. Why do they hate us?....another one of your genius leaders asks. No…it is not because of your freedoms. Your freedoms will come our way soon enough. We see it in our children. They love your way of life all too well. It will be impossible to stem this tide forever. And it is not because of our religion. Islam has been co-opted in this war. It is only a factor in the sense that religion has been the rallying cry of the dispossessed since time immemorial. Don't put our religion on trial. Walk softly…I was going to complete the idiom…and carry a big stick…no need….just walk softly America." Dr. al Ghanim concluded his sermon.

Because I was leaving the next morning, Mustapha insisted he personally take me back to the hotel after dinner. We had decided to stop at Starbucks again before the drop off. As we got out of the car, I noticed a group of four men… distinctly American military looking…. actually Navy Seal looking …I thought to myself…..getting into the adjacent car. I couldn't be sure, but one of them looked awfully familiar to me. I did a double take. "Bones?....David Bonner?....is that you?" I called out. He turned and made eye contact. This was definitely my classmate from Bowdoin. Yes, there were at least twenty years in between, but some faces change slowly. There was no question I was face to face with my old friend Bones. He looked startled…bewildered?...and then without a word, slid into the back seat of the car and it sped off.

"That was weird," I said as much to myself as to Mustapha. "Who were those guys?" I was still reeling from the snub. "Great question," he replied. "None of us are too sure. We keep pretty close tabs on American military personnel on our soil. It's part of the deal. For the most part they are confined to the base itself. But these guys are different. They have been granted some kind of diplomatic immunity from on high. To be honest, it's a bit of a mystery to our military command what they're doing here. Your brass have sequestered an old abandoned fishing/pearl diving village about two hours south of the city. These guys are based there. The security is unbelievable, even by your standards. Whatever they're up to, clearly your government doesn't want the rest of the world to know about it," Mustapha exclaimed.

We pulled up in front of my hotel. "So on your next visit Alec, I'd like you to bring along some samples of these *exoskeletons* your R&D guys have been working on; astonishing really. Imagine by simply donning one of these suits…our skinny Kuwaiti soldiers turning into cyborgs!" the colonel joked. "I'll do the best I can Mustapha, but I can imagine that our Israeli friends will have something to say about that!" It was an appropriately light-hearted way to close out one of the more bizarre of my forays into the 'modern' Arab world.

CHAPTER 9

THE WAR ON TERROR

With the neo-cons in power in the wake of 9/11, the principle of pre-emptive war gained traction in America. Any threat to America would be headed off at the pass, so to speak. This philosophy, was neatly summarized by the National Security Director, with her "searching for the *smoking gun"* metaphor. "If the smoking gun turns out to be a mushroom cloud... well..." But with the war in Iraq, not going quite as planned, and democracy not blossoming or flourishing as designed, a different kind of warfare was being considered.

With Al Quaeda, Al Shabab and other miscellaneous, unfriendly to America entities, establishing toeholds in failed or failing states around the globe, the war theatre itself had become global. The Geneva Convention had become a little outdated...passe, argued the deep thinkers of the neo-con movement. America was at war with stateless actors. Rules of engagement involving detention without charge, coercive intelligence gathering...read torture...and general respect for civil liberties, had to be re-examined in light of this new type of warfare. Modern technology fused with this modern mode of battle, in the form of "targeted killings" by missile guided drones. Our industry was hard at work trying to keep pace with the changing face of war.

Assassinations, political or otherwise, were nothing new in the American lexicon and practice of defending American interests around the globe. Such covert warfare had been waged by American governments successfully on all continents for decades. 9/11 was the perfect cover for the neo cons to intensify the practice. In a way, it was a coup for Bud, as Vice President, to be granted responsibility and control over the new entity .....*Joint Special Operations Command.* Answering only to the White House, unlike the CIA, this tiny, efficient, para-military unit, would be able to hide in the shadows...away from the glare of Congressional oversight...from burdensome public scrutiny, and, when duty calls, carry out some of the more nefarious but necessary actions, that the general public might find morally indigestible. JSOC would prove very useful. No doubt the Founding Fathers would have frowned at such an affront to their Constitution and potential harm to civil liberties guaranteed within...but then again, could the Founding Fathers have imagined an enemy like Al Qaeda? Such went the thinking...or rationalization.

But what a mess Iraq had become. Fear and feelings of vengeance after 9/11, had given way to fatigue, anger, and a return to a more isolationist world outlook, on the part of the American public. People felt manipulated and lied to by their leaders. The neo cons had their chance and they blew it. As previously described, the boot had been readied, and 2008 was the kickoff! Good-bye Mr. President, good-bye Bud, good-bye Mr. Rumsfeld, good-bye Mr. Wolfowitz. And then flight 867 and the fear…and Bud…returned. When the Republicans were returned to power, JSOC survived, but in a new form. It had become Bud's personal army, and he would have at least another four years to wield it in any way he chose. Dangerous?… yes…but was anyone paying attention?….not yet.

I came through the door of my apartment and was reminded of the domestic mess I had left behind in the panic of getting to the airport on time a week before. Half a cup of cold coffee, toast crumbs and an egg-encrusted plate still waited to be cleared. It would have to wait. I crawled into my unmade bed and flipped off the light. As an afterthought I pushed the button on my voicemail. A couple of cold calls selling insurance and duct cleaning, and a welcome home greeting from my mother and I was almost off to sleep….and then Bud. I almost didn't recognize the voice. Slow…leaden….medicated? "Alec…how are you?…Bud here….listen, any chance you could rally the boys for a hike up to the lodge? I really need to get out of Washington for a bit, and I thought it might be a chance to pick up where we left off a couple months ago. I haven't been myself lately, and I could really use the break. I realize you guys have heavy schedules and commitments too, so it's probably a long shot. Anyway…. give it some thought…check with Mac and Suds if you're up for it. Best time would be two weekends from now. Let me know if you will be in Washington. I can get the Ranger to pick you up and drop you off on the island. No hassle. Hope all is well."

I checked the nightstand clock. Midnight…too late to call Suds? I dialed the number. A couple of rings and then, "Alec…what's up," Suds slurred in baritone sleepiness, "I thought you were in the Middle East." "Just got back. Look Suds, sorry to call so late. Hope I didn't wake the family," I offered apologetically, "but I just got in and there was a message from Bud. He didn't sound great and he wanted to know if Mac, you and me could join him at the lodge Friday next. I know it's ridiculously short notice, but I'm going to juggle my schedule. I haven't talked to Mac yet. What do you think?" "What do you mean he didn't sound great?" Suds asked. "Is he alright?" "Probably I'm reading too much into it. I just thought he sounded a bit strange…a little morose that's all," I replied. "Ok, well look…I'll have to clear it with Jen in the morning. But check with Mac. If he can make it, I'll do my best not to let you down," Suds graciously, if tentatively responded. "Ok…will do….sorry again to wake you up," I apologized. "But one more thing before you go," Suds added, "how are we going to get there… dogsled? I don't relish the idea of ploughing through two feet of ice and snow, a la Amundsen. You know I'm not the adventuresome type!" "No worries…the copter will pick us up and set us down…boring," I replied. "Ok….I like boring," Suds signed off.

A quick check with Mac the next day and a thumbs up by Suds, and we were good to go. I emailed confirmation to Bud right away, as I could imagine that there would be more than a little security protocol involved, in even a simple weekend getaway by the Vice President. I was looking forward to a more relaxed reunion this time. But there was something in Bud's voice that suggested that this may not be the rollicking good times that usually took place when the four of us gathered for a weekend.

CHAPTER 10

A SINFUL BOND

There had been a light dusting of snow overnight, and as the copter touched down it threw up a blizzard of icy chrystals that forced me to cover my face with my scarf, as I boarded. The plan was to pick up Mac and Suds in Boston, and then continue from there to the lodge in Maine. I was not surprised to learn that both had made difficult adjustments to their schedules to make our weekend possible. Over the years, we had relied heavily on each other when bumps appeared on our respective paths. That's what friends do right? As the suburbs of Maryland faded into the distance and the landscape below became less differentiated…a whiteout of open, snow-covered hills and fields….my mind drifted back to the circumstances, twenty-five years earlier, when fate….destiny?….tied my future so tightly to Bud's.

Given the four of us had such great fun as classmates, roommates and sports-mates, over our time together at Milton, we had decided…. why not keep it going? Why not do our undergraduate together at Bowdoin; great school and four more years of adolescent, goofball hijinks and fraternity frivolity together? But there was one catch….me! For the others, admission to Bowdoin, as respected an institution of higher learning as it was, was a slam-dunk. Mac and Suds' academic achievements and Bud's social preeminence and connections, virtually guaranteed it. Although my scores would be considered borderline for admission, the bigger hurdle for me was the cost. But there was always the possibility of athletic scholarship. With persistent hope, we nursed the concept of continued fraternity, post high school, through the final months at Milton, and kept our dream of togetherness alive.

You could cloak the misstep…the transgression…the sin…whatever your moral or spiritual code directs….in religious garb; the devil made me do it….irresistible fruit….the original sin. But thinking back, it wasn't deserving of attribution to a higher power. It was mortal weakness of the most prosaic….pure and simple. I couldn't handle the pressure. Or even worse; I got lazy and reached for the low-hanging fruit.

The coaches at Bowdoin had made it clear. As much as they wanted to recruit my talents and include me in their hockey program, their influence with their admissions people was limited. My SAT scores were acceptable. If I could just get my GPA a few points higher, their job would be a lot easier and a scholarship would be more attainable. And then the heavens opened....and lo and behold....the Geography exam appeared on Mr. Dickenson's desk. His main job was Head of the Counselling Department, but he doubled as a Geography teacher. I had come into his office to attend to a detail in my university application. He wasn't present, so I had decided to wait for him. Eve had offered up the "poison fruit" in the form of a finished draft of the year end exam, sitting on a platter in the middle of his desk. I stepped into the hallway and looked both ways....not a soul in sight. How many calculations is the human brain capable of in two seconds? I either made a million or I made none. Fast-forward to the examination room. I had never been this nervous. This was overtime, game seven in hockey parlance and then some. I set my graphics calculator off to one side and called up the exam solutions. If I had done rapid computer-like calculations before the crime, one of them should have been the probability that any of the exam supervisors would be up to date with the potential of this new information storage technology. I looked around the exam room. Why didn't I just preserve this opportunity for myself? It was a miscalculation to be so unselfish to be sure. Too many of my friends were showing too much reliance on their calculators in a Geography exam! I sensed the game might be over. I was right....hellfire awaited me.

I thought it was a stroke of genius and evidence of Bud's loyalty and generosity in friendship. Others suggested, unkindly, it was typical Bud, exploiting an opportunity to display the power and influence of his family's position in the school community, as he did too often for their liking. Either way, there was no doubt he rescued my future and I would be forever in his debt. When it was clear our gooses were cooked and ready to be served up in a Headmasterial, inquisitorial feast, Bud called the group together. His plan was simple but our stories had to be in sync. Bud had been the mastermind in the crime. Bud removed the exam and had it copied before returning it, undetected, back to Mr. Dickinson's desk. Bud had shared the contents with the other accused. Bud would take the fall. But the plan required no wavering...no dissenters...were we all in? And mysteriously the crime evaporated into thin air. It was as if it didn't happen. Faced with a choice between the potential evaporation of millions of dollars in endowment campaign funding which the O'Dwyer family had recently pledged and a morally responsible reaction to dishonorable conduct....well, you guessed it.... it was the crime that disappeared; the funding remained intact.

I recall it as the darkest days of my life. I couldn't sleep. Night after night, I lay awake in a cold sweat. I imagined the worst. University doors would be closed to a convicted cheater. The Bowdoin doors for certain were impregnable. Over and over in my mind they slammed shut with an ugly, bone jarring finality. But it was the potential shame to my family that created the most hellish agony. How could I face my father? Bud could handle it. There was something about urbanite sophistication that made such dishonor easier to bear. I asked Bud about this. He was dismissive. Sure his parents would be disappointed, but they would view it as a poor choice in the recklessness of youth. He even joked that in the Catholic world of levellized sin, it wasn't that big a deal…venial at worst, in his estimation. Not so in small town, rural America. There was no place to hide from shame in a small community.

And then it passed. A tidy bow to cap off the whole unsavory affair, came in the form of the scholarship and acceptance letter from Bowdoin. Was this the destiny my father spoke of? Was I truly in control? In hindsight, one might think I learned my lesson. I had strayed from the moral path laid out for me by my right-living parents. But if this could be seen as a fork in my life's journey, I took the road most travelled. I followed the money. The lesson I came away with, would have disappointed my father. Maybe we *were* in control of our destinies. But one thing was clear to me. It was a hell of a lot more likely with enough cash in your pocket!

CHAPTER 11

———————— •◆• ————————

THE LODGE

With Mac and Suds on board and the Ranger negotiating the final few kilometers of lakes and hills before touchdown on the island, my thoughts turned to the sheer beauty and isolation of the wintry landscape below. To be dropped by copter into the north woods this time of year, was no small advantage. In fact it was often touch and go whether the lodge was accessible in any other way in deep winter. Leaving aside the potential hazards of crossing the ice-covered lake to reach the homestead, the narrow country roads were often inaccessible…bathtubs of drifting snow between the granite rock faces that loomed on either side and ushered you to your remote destination.

"Looks so different in winter," Mac announced, as the island with the lodge peeking out from the pines at its highest point, appeared in our line of vision. "I hope Bud called ahead to get the heat on….looks a little frigid down there," Suds commented. "If he didn't, at least the beer should be nice and cold," I joked. Of course Bud's travels (probably even to the corner store) were meticulously orchestrated. Not only would the heat be on, but it was almost guaranteed that we would be welcomed by a crackling fire in the hearth, a well-stocked pantry and plenty of cold beer, Jack Daniels, or any other ibation that our little hearts or habits, desired.

We piled out on touchdown, bags in tow, crouching against the swirling snow thrown up by the copter's blades. "Bundle up," the pilot had warned on parting. "Minus 25 out there." The twenty-five feet to the front entrance was just within the limits of endurance of our Washington-pampered, citified constitutions. Bud was waiting at the door. "Hey boys… welcome to God's country. Glad you could make it."

The lodge itself was a spectacularly warm refuge from the elements without. As predicted, a roaring fire in the floor to towering ceiling, stone fireplace, greeted our arrival. The timber-frame skeleton of three hundred year-old hand-hewn posts and beams was breathtaking. I rubbed my hand along a gargantuan, soft, pine post that delineated the living space….a tactile history lesson I thought to myself; perhaps the handiwork of Bud's great grandparents with some help from the natives.

"Thanks for making the effort guys…it really means a lot to me. What can I get you to drink?" Bud offered. "A little early maybe…but as they say…it's twelve o'clock somewhere," he added lightly. Mac and Suds would later confirm my first thought on seeing Bud only a few months since the funeral. He had visibly aged. There were lines and dark pouches under his eyes that made him look like he was recovering from an all-night bender.

We had pulled our chairs round the fireplace and caught up on jobs and families and the minutiae of our respective careers when Bud announced the plan for the afternoon. "Ok boys…in keeping with my general philosophy that there is no free lunch in America, I have arranged that we will "catch" our dinners tonight! I had a flashback to that rabbit in the crosshairs, earlier in the story. What the hell. It was good to get out of the city, and revel in the simple life, but I wasn't prepared for the challenge of taking down an elk with a shotgun… or harpooning a bear for my dinner. I noticed the antique rifles hanging from the timbers, and the majestic buck's head with its cascading rack of antlers. "Bud…you're not serious… American Sniper I am not!" I jokingly pleaded. "Ha ha….wait and see Alec. I guarantee you won't starve, despite your bad aim and woodland rustiness. Daniel Boone or not, I assure you we will eat well tonight."

After climbing a hand-crafted, log, spiral staircase and depositing our bags in our respective bedrooms, Bud directed us to a mud-room towards the back of the lodge. Winter-wear that Daniel Boone could never dream of, and that would make our primitive quest for dinner relatively painless, was hanging on hooks. We would be warm as NASA bugs in a rug, in these futuristic fibres, some of them no doubt, products of my own company's laboratories. I smiled at the obvious ironies of this mission. If our weapons were equally up to date…well… the wildlife wouldn't stand a chance!

Several snowmobiles were waiting for us as we came out the back of the lodge. One had a trailer loaded with an ice cooler and what looked to me like fish tackle. Hunting for frozen fish seemed an easier gambit than trying to take down the hoppers and jumpers of the wild, I amused myself thinking. Engines fired up, an affront to the pristine quiet of the woods, and we started down the trail. It occurred to me that we had yet to see any evidence of national security anywhere on the island. Without a doubt they were there; just sufficiently professional to grant the privacy that Bud demanded.

We pulled up in front of the ice hut and engines off, the silence of the wild returned. "Grab that beer cooler will you Mac," Bud called out, his breath visible in the arctic-temperature air. I helped unclasp the fishing tackle and we dragged our equipment through the tiny door.

"Welcome to Chez O'Dwyer," Bud announced with flair. "All you can eat….but you have to catch it first is the rule," he added with a chuckle. Like everything else in our tour so far, the stage had been set before we arrived. Four chairs were arranged around a dark eight inch hole in the ice, and a miniature oil heater took the chill off and made our space suits somewhat redundant. "Fishing just for dinner is a little dull for me," Bud declared. "Longest catch gets to ante in for free in tonight's game," he added. And with that he helped each of us, attach our hooks and lures and get our lines in the water.

The *call of the wild*, a primeval instinct, seemed to be common to many cultures around the world. Whether it was western urbanites fleeing to the lakeside cottage on weekends, or modern Arabs, retreating to desert compounds in an attempt to reconnect with their Bedouin roots, the urge seemed to be irresistible. Suds might be the authority on this. It was psychological. A yearning for a simpler existence; a retreat from the complexities and hectic demands of the too fast-paced, modern world. It was a human longing. As the four of us sat, huddled together in this ten by ten hut, expectantly silent before our fishing lines, I couldn't help but think that for Bud, there was a deeper longing at stake. We were participants in his mourning. He was caught between two worlds; not between the bucolic and the frenetic, but rather between this life and the afterlife. In our conversation and reminiscences, it was clear that Stephen was never far from his mind. A tug on Mac's line and with surprising deftness he hauled an iridescent, flopping, pickerel onto the ice before his feet. "Not bad," Bud offered. "An hors d'oeuvre at least," he chided.

The abiding friendship between Mac and Bud always puzzled me. They could hardly have been any more different in their personalities and their views of the world. Bud was brash… Mac was reserved. Bud had swagger…Mac had scholarship. Mac's currency was history… Bud's currency was….well…currency. Mac believed in the progress of history….in learning from history. Bud believed in America…more specifically the power of America. There was clearly a mutual respect. It was just never clear to me what each respected in the other. Over the years, there was never a shortage of collisions…head-on car crashes of opinions between the two of them. But somehow their friendship endured. It was impressive to me.

The pull on my line caught me by surprise. I lost at least ten feet of line before I recovered. "Now that has the makings of a main course," Bud exclaimed. "Easy does it….patience…. it's almost in the pan…add a little oil…and presto!….my Moby Dick came thrashing to the surface and was quickly netted by Bud. "Dinner is served," he jested. A beautiful twelve inch lake trout was added to the menu.

The Iraq debacle should have been the end of their friendship, I thought at the time. Mac had been dead on about the aftermath of the invasion. He couldn't have called it any more precisely. But his voice wasn't heard. Bud had declared Mac's thesis politely, as one of several possible scenarios, and then impolitely dismissed it on Meet the Press, declaring that he was sure Americans would be treated as liberators by appreciative Iraqis. I asked Mac if he wasn't hurt by his friend's vote of non-confidence. His response was remarkably Christ-like for such a total non-Christian, I thought. "He knows not what he does?" Mac retorted. He sees the world the way he was taught to see it. I didn't give him the answer he wanted or needed, that's all."

Without verbalizing it, I was confident that Mac and Suds understood that this weekend was part of the healing process. It was about reconnecting with past lives…it was about Stephen. I had hoped we could stay on task. On the other hand, we were leisurely passing time with one of the foremost movers and shakers on the planet. Even Suds, whose business was entirely apolitical, could hardly resist an inside scoop regarding the direction Bud and his pals were taking the country. But Mac was first to break ranks.

"Bud, without giving away state secrets, do you think the Iran deal will come together," Mac asked, maybe a bit too pointedly. "I hope not," Bud replied curtly. I looked to see if he was putting us on, but he was focused on his line and a sign of an imminent catch. I looked at both Mac and Suds and they were equally flummoxed by the reply. If you were American, you were fully aware of the political capital the President had invested in this deal. Mac was not about to let it go. "Are you serious?" he probed. But Bud was concentrating on his lure. He snapped his line and set the hook on his dinner. "Hey…I'm not sure I'll be able to eat all of this baby," he boasted. "Suds you may have to help me," he wasn't exaggerating, as a five or six pound bass was corralled in his net.

His winning catch in safe-keeping, Bud resumed the conversation. "Look….Mac…you're a smart guy. What are the two gravest threats to the world at the moment." Before he had a chance to answer, Bud continued. "Nuclear weapons and theocracies…beyond question." "Any disagreement?" he challenged. Mac didn't disagree. "Now put them together and what do you have?" was Bud's follow up question. "A nightmare….Armageddon….the twelfth Imam (also referred to as the Hidden Imam who would make his appearance in the end of times)….the end of the world." "But isn't that what this deal is addressing?" Mac queried. "That's what the President believes," Bud answered. "But you don't?" Mac was being cautious. "This deal kicks the can down the road, that's all. It buys us time. But by the time the deal expires we will have not one, but three theocracies on our hands. One Sunni…one Shia…and one Judaic.

And there is every chance all three will have nuclear capabilities...of course one already does. I happen to think we are better off getting down to business now."

My eyes met Mac's. He looked astonished...bewildered....frightened? The fishing hut had become uncomfortably claustrophobic for the three of us. Of course the elephant in the room, was the dangerous, mind-boggling possibility, that the President and Vice-President could have competing agendas. This is not the way our country worked. Was it?

CHAPTER 12

RASPUTIN REVEALED

The seven fishes (yes it had been a productive afternoon in the hunter and gatherer department) sautéed in an expensive chianti and consumed, we had retired in front of the fireplace in an after dinner repose. "Ah the life of the blessed," Suds remarked. "So nice to step away from the anxieties of the human condition if only for a brief reprise," he added a little sardonically. "I haven't felt this relaxed in some time." I glanced at Mac. He was looking less than relaxed despite the opportunity. I knew he was still stewing over Bud's earlier revelation of possible disharmony at the highest level of governance in the land. I knew he couldn't let it go. Bud was puffing away on an after-dinner cigar, lost in thought .no doubt on the subject of his bereavement. One reminiscence after another in the fishing hut, throughout the afternoon, inevitably segued to Stephen and the delights and discoveries that he and Bud had shared in their magic moments at the lodge. Please Mac, respect our friend's state of mind.

A log snapped in the fire and sent a burst of sparks onto the hearth, as if an authorization for Mac to disturb the calm. "Surely to God Bud, you don't think we can wrestle Islam… the religion of merely a couple of billion souls on the planet… to the ground. How do you propose we deal with these "dangerous" theocracies? There is no way but to engage them, surely." Jesus Mac, I thought to myself. You ass. This is not the time or place.

Bud took a long puff on his cigar. He didn't seem particularly perturbed or surprised by Mac's challenge. I considered the possibility that Bud had deliberately set the hook in Mac's contrarian worldview. Their friendship had the aspect of the alter-ego. Bud needed to tune in to Mac's wavelength, even if it was his habit to ignore the message. "Why do you say Islam Mac? You weren't listening. Judaism is just as dangerous. The Jews have a Masada complex. As the world squeezes Israel, as the ugly, racist, pariah state they have become, they will retreat to a fortress of the Orthodox. It's happening as we speak. The big difference between the Jews of 70 AD, and the current Jews, is they have an option beyond mass suicide. They have the potential to take the rest of the world with them. In terms of theocracies and their threat to our way of life, it is only a question of which one to deal with first. In that sense, you are right. Islam is the first on the list."

Mac looked flabbergasted. "And just how do you suppose to eradicate a fifteen hundred year-old religion….no less than the culture of almost a third of the human race?" He responded in disbelief. "Oh Mac. I wish I was half as learned and half as clever as you." Bud conceded. "You know the depth and the power of the hatred and differences within the faith. You should have received some kind of award for the quality and prescience of your scholarship, before Iraq. If we had listened to you, we could have saved a lot of American lives. But live and learn. We won't make the same mistake twice, if I have anything to say about it. You are absolutely right if you're suggesting that this is beyond the military and economic might of the world's greatest power. America can't do it….but Islam can. You haven't considered the logical extension of your scholarship….the cannabilization of the faith. Let the Sunnis and Shias do what we can't. American foreign policy must be targeted at facilitating the desired outcome. We'll supply the means and sit back and watch the show. The wisdom and beauty of such an approach must be obvious to anyone paying attention."

As previously noted, I had a tendency to filter ideas through the wires of my company's share prices. Bud's American foreign policy thesis was causing haywire in my networks! What the fuck did all this mean! Mac was blanching in utter astonishment. Like me, he couldn't square the content. If Bud were Zeus on a mountaintop, and there were more than a few suggestions in the back channels in Washington that he was, there was a lightning bolt emanating from his staff. This was insane. Almost in a whisper Mac asked, "Is this the current, official, foreign policy position of the United States of America?" Only silence met the question.

"I'm going to go for a walk," Bud broke the tension. "You guys relax here in front of the fire, and when I get back, we'll have a couple of liqueurs and get the game going." He grabbed his hat and parka, pulled on his boots and was out the door. Mac erupted. "Jesus Alec….tell me he wasn't serious! Facilitate mutual ethnic cleansing? That's a fuck of a new concept! I mean for Christ's sake….this is sheer madness! It scares the shit outta me." "Look…Mac… relax. We don't know everything that goes on in the ivory tower of the White House, but my industry keeps pretty close tabs on *the lay of the land*, shall we say. I can assure you no such *"final solution"* to the radicalism of Islam has been even whispered in our corridors," was the best I could offer. Suds weighed in. "Mac, despite the outward appearances of normalcy today, I picked up lots of indication that Bud is still under enormous stress. It's not my specialty, but I would say, though his grief is not laid bare, it is there, roiling beneath the surface. I would take Bud's curious revelation with that in mind." "Curious! You call that shit curious?" Mac was beside himself. "It is exactly Bud's state of mind that is cause for alarm, for Christ' sake," he whined. "Stay put guys. I think I'll join him outside. Keep the home fires burning. I'll be right back." I grabbed my coat and went out into the arctic air.

I found Bud on one of his favorite perches….a rocky outcropping that offered a panoramic view of the lake. Given the sheer fifty foot drop from the edge, I made sure I didn't startle him. He was clearly lost in thought. "Beautiful out here isn't it Bud?" I began carefully. "I don't remember the last time I saw a sky this black. It's not just the bright lights of Washington that ruin the show. I'm pretty sure all that hot air keeps the stars from shimmering too," I added in a weak attempt at humour. "I don't know how many nights Stevie and I use to sit on this very edge and try to take it all in. When he was seven or eight, I tried to use it as a science lesson. Not just the names of the constellations, but I'd ask him….how many stars do you think there are up there Stevie? How far do you think it is to the edge of the universe? I remember he said, what do you mean the edge Daddy? Is there a last station where we get off? He was such a smart kid. You know I think there are some concepts…infinity for example…. that kids with their wonderfully elastic imaginations, grasp more thoroughly than adults. Our imaginations atrophy over time…with every disappointment, every compromised ideal, every exposure to the harsh realities of human flaws and frailties….we lose it bit by bit. We're forced to deal with the world as it is. Not always as pretty as this night sky eh Alec?" I considered he might be alluding to my chosen career as an arms peddler….probably not…just my own moral insecurities, I thought to myself. I waited for him to continue. "I miss him so much. God how I miss him. You know it sounds strange, but the weeks following the funeral, I have never been so close to him. He was with me everywhere I went. He slept curled up next to me….we had breakfast together….he sat at the table during national security briefings….he spoke to me….he challenged my choices…Dad are you sure about this?….he never left my side. But I can feel him slipping away. He's gone missing lately. He's not there when I wake up in the morning. His voice is growing weaker. Alec…I'm really scared. I don't know if I can keep going without him." I put my arm around my best friend. I could feel him quaking with emotion. The frozen tears of Rasputin rained forth. The Vice President of the United States of America was broken.

CHAPTER 13

A PERSIAN PUTSCH

Why do they hate us?....uh....let me count the ways. In 1953 the popular and democratically elected Prime Minister of Iran, Mohammed Mossadegh asked the Anglo-Iranian Oil Company, the antecedent of the present day BP, British Petroleum, to open the company's books to government inspection. The Brits told Mr. Mossadegh to go to hell. The Prime Minister responded by nationalizing the entire oil industry, much to his people's delight. The Brits responded with an operation, largely led and financed by the CIA, with the charmingly creative title of "Operation Boot". For our part, we Americans gained control over a healthy chunk of the vast Iranian oil reserves. For their part, the Iranians got Mohammed-Rezza Shah Pahlavi, the infamous Shah of Iran, who effectively ruled for the next twenty-five years as an absolute monarch. American weapons and the CIA-trained, notorious secret police, the Savak, ensured peace, prosperity (for some) and repression throughout the land. Do they hate us for our freedoms?...uh....I think it is just as likely they hate us for screwing with *their* freedom! Anyway, as any casual student of American history knows, there was a straight path to the return of the mullahs, and the hostage taking of 1979. I can't help but think that if President Carter's covert attempt to free the American Embassy hostages, had gone as well as the JSOC takeout of Bin Laden last year, the recent history of America would have been written much differently. Those damn dust storms in the desert; hard to factor in contingencies when God gets involved.

Contingencies were at the heart of the present day *Operation Boot*. The plan this time was more modest in scope. Success meant not booting the government, but booting the deal. Like advances in medical surgery, we Americans had come a long way in the past thirty years, in the business of sneaky, surgical strikes of political motive. It wasn't just the futuristic technology that defined our reach, but equally critical, our gathering of actionable intelligence. For example, in Bushehr, on this bright, sunny May morning, Bud's army didn't just know the personal schedule of Ibrahim Mansour, head of Iran's nuclear energy ministry, they knew his favourite hotel and the most likely route he would travel to the Bushehr nuclear plant. That was the easy part. The hard part was having enough contingencies in place to hide from the world that this was an operation undertaken not by America…but by America's shadow government. This was Bud's play…these were Bud's boys in play. "This Bud's for You" would have been an appropriate slogan for the operation. And if the world and his boss, ever found out…well…the fallout for Bud would be nuclear.

Given that Israel equally abhorred the impending nuclear deal, it would seem to have made sense for Bud to consider a joint venture. After-all, the Mossad had proven to be the masters of this kind of mayhem. Since 2007, Mossad agents on motor-cycles, had taken out five Iranian scientists, sticking magnetically-attachable bombs to their victim's cars. But secrecy trumped collusion and it made more sense to use the Israelis as cover, rather than include them in the mission. The Muslim world had a knee-jerk reaction to every spurious global event these days. They blamed everything on Israel. It also helped that under pressure from the American President to *please* stop killing Iranian scientists, (Americans always say please when it comes to Israel) while the deal was being formulated, the Israeli Prime Minister Benjamin Netanyahu, indicated that they had decided it was too dangerous to continue anyway. They worried about having their best spies captured and hanged. Ergo…the perfect alibi. 'Bones' Bonner spoke perfect Hebrew. Speaking of Bones, he may not have had the balls of a suicide bomber….the conviction regarding virgins in heaven….but you had to give it to him…he was a true patriot. Not everyone can go about their work, knowing it is the job of the guy behind him to put a bullet in his head if anything goes awry! So when Bud's crew set sail, just before dawn, from their Kuwaiti training ground, in their space-age stealth submarine pod, there was no slight trepidation involved. And despite the best laid plans of mice and men, things did go awry.

Bones and his back-up assassin, headed out into the chaotic traffic of downtown Bushehr the next morning, on their Iranian motorbikes, as planned. They received confirmation from their handlers, via drones over the Arabian Gulf, that Mr. Mansour was right on schedule. With Navy Seal, James Bond- like precision and stealth, Bones calmly and inconspicuously maneuvered alongside the silver BMW, with the unsuspecting Dr. Mansour inside and attached the Israeli-made explosives. With only five seconds to detonation, he accelerated away from the car.

Despite endless repetitions and rehearsals of the scene….drill after drill after drill…once the payload is delivered there is *no looking back*…literally. Escape is everything. But as it goes with curiosity and cats, Bones Bonner, on feeling the impact of the blast on his back, could not resist a peek over his shoulder. He refocused just in time to catch the fruit vendor in his rickety three wheeler, cross into his flight path. It was the last thing he would remember. Mr. Bonner's personal assassin tried frantically to navigate through the ensuing bedlam and draw nearer to his kill. He raised his weapon as per his duty to erase the evidentiary trail, when he felt an arm around his neck, and three revolutionary guards relieved him of his responsibilities. As per training, he bit down hard on the cyanide pill. His mission had ended.

Depending on which version of the tale you subscribed to, Bones' mission would continue a little longer. If not for the information- gathering possibilities of the psychoactive medication sodium pentothal, more commonly referred to as truth serum, the Iranian fury in the aftermath of the slaying of their nuclear energy boss, might well have been directed at Israel. As it was, you might say the mission had been fifty per cent successful. A familiar scene; Iranians took to the streets in droves, burning American flags, chanting death to America, America is Satan; a national outpouring of disgust and venom directed at American hypocrisy. The impending nuclear deal had been atomized. On the other hand, the failure of the other fifty per cent of the mission….leaving no trail of responsibility….shook the nation in unimaginable ways. It wouldn't just spell the end of Bud's political life and mission. It would spell the end of the Patriot Act itself. In the following weeks, as the full extent of the abuse of trust and power of Bud's office came to light, the nation recoiled in anger and disbelief. How could this happen?

Of course there were no shortage of pundits who *after the fact*, saw it coming. Bud had always been the Rasputin of the American court. He represented the dark, sinister side of the American government, plotting and scheming in the shadows, through three consecutive terms. His counsel to the President was always given privately. He trusted few and few trusted him. But Americans had fallen asleep on the watch. Maybe the constitution didn't recognize and address this potentially harmful and dangerous, concentration of power in the Vice Presidency, but someone should have noticed. Finally, when the CIA and FBI dug deeper and uncovered evidence of Bud's secret war with Islam….his manifesto of facilitated intra-religious annihilation, the apparent state of his mind and the scale of his crime, caused the nation to gasp in disbelief. Mad with grief or simply mad, Bud was not deemed a sympathetic character in this play. He had acted against his country. He was guilty of treason.

CHAPTER 14

ISLAM OR BEDLAM

A year had passed since the devastating, heart-breaking image of Bud, being escorted in handcuffs from the Oval Office by agents from the FBI. His facial expression has been etched in my memory….passive, vacant…a kind of Forrest Gump innocent bewilderment in his eyes. News reports speculated about the results of the compulsory psychiatric testing that would precede his trial. Given that his defense team had indicated they would file a plea of not guilty by reason of insanity, much depended on the medical reporting. Both Suds and Mac were in Washington on this day, and we had agreed to meet for lunch.

A heavy spring downpour soaked my dress shirt and pants as I made the dash from cab to restaurant entrance. Mac and Suds were already seated and were working on their first ale. "Hey guys…great to see you again. Beautiful day huh?" I kidded as I slid into the booth. "How are things?" "Good Alec," they responded in unison, "What's new in the war industry...things humming along?" Mac never missed a chance for a dig. "Hah…ya…never been better. You know how it works Mac. As the world goes to hell in a hand basket, my bank account gets healthier and healthier. Things are really looking up!" After placing our orders, we turned to the obvious topic. "Suds, I guess you heard about Bud's defense plea. Has this ever been argued successfully? Can grief lead to insanity?" I asked. "I don't know that it's ever been tried in a court of law, but there is substantial literature on the subject," Suds responded. "No consensus though. Insanity itself is not as clear cut a concept as you might think. It is resistant to easy, clinical definition." "You know it occurs to me that the neo-cons, some of Bud's closet associates, are undermining his legal defense, by rushing to the defense of his premise. Rather than suggesting evidence of insanity, the idea of an isolationist America, providing the weapons and watching from the sidelines, as the Islamic world devours itself, is being considered as their central foreign policy tenet. They have proclaimed it genius rather than insanity! Maybe Bud's lawyers will have to take the tact that there is a fine line between the two," Mac offered insincerely.

"Isn't it ironic that Hassan's defense team quit over this issue. They wanted to file an insanity plea, but the Major refused. He wanted to plead guilty and get his just reward; paradise as a martyr!" Mac added. "Some of the court filings were made public just recently.

He spoke very matter of factly about his motivation and his crime. It was very clear he killed for his God. It was a religious obligation in his version of Islam."

"You know Mac, this is one thing we have always been in fairly close agreement on. I accept your scholarly view that Islam needs time to adjust to the modern world. We have to support the moderates. I get that. But we may run out of time don't you think? I mean I read the other day that eighty-four per cent of Pakistanis want to see Sharia as the law of the land. I don't have to remind you that Pakistan is a nuclear power. The stoning of adulterers, unbelievers and homosexuals is hardly consistent with human rights in the 21st century. How long are we supposed to wait?" I asked rhetorically.

"Well." Mac responded, "I read the same poll and you forgot to mention that only twelve per cent of Turks, and Turkey is largely a homogeneous Muslim country, wanted anything to do with Sharia. But I agree that it is hard to see how Sharia can survive in an enlightened society. All I can do is point to signs of progress. Look at Egypt and how General al-Sisi is trying to address the radicalism. He is calling for a "religious revolution" and is planning to use the scholars and clerics of Al-Azhar, the one thousand year old centre for Islamic learning, to preach moderation. He basically said to them, *you Imams are responsible before Allah. The entire world is waiting. The entire world is waiting for your next word because our nation is being torn apart.* There is a long way to go, I agree, but what are the alternatives. Bud's thinking *was* insane…. annihilation of Islam? Who needs the end of times? This is apocalyptic enough!"

Both Mac and Suds knew I had been trying for months, through my connections at the Pentagon, to get permission to visit Bud. I surprised them with the announcement that I had secured permission for a short visit later this very afternoon. In the taxi to the court prison, I recalled Sud's comment on hearing about the visit. "I should warn you Alec that you can't expect to be greeted by the Bud we knew. I have been privy to his medical reports and there is every chance he may not even recognize you. It might be an uphill battle to prove he was unstable at the time of his alleged crimes, but there is apparently little doubt about his current state of mind."

I prepared myself the best I could, but when the prison guard drew the bolt and opened the door to Bud's cell, I considered for a moment a hasty retreat. He was sitting on the edge of his bed in the eight by ten, concrete bunker, staring at the floor. He raised his head as I came in. "Stevie? Is that you Stevie?" he asked. I had read about stress-related dementia, but I had never experienced it first-hand. I was at a total loss. Bud had aged markedly. I paused…and then…"ya Dad….how are you keeping? Are they looking after you ok?" He didn't answer me. "Stevie….how far is it to the edge of the moral universe?" "Is that a trick question Dad?" I thought he looked through me. His eyes were empty. I paused again. "I guess that would depend on whether you believed the arc bent towards justice," I answered. "Ha!" he startled me. "That's my boy. You always were a clever boy Stevie." He continued, "I tell you Stevie…. all you ever need to know about life you can find in Shakespeare…did you know that?"

"You remember Dad. I hated Shakespeare. I failed that course." I didn't know how long I could go on with this. And then, without warning, he rose slowly from his cot and walked past me to the door as if I wasn't there. It was barely more than a whisper, but I remembered the lines. With his back to me….staring through the bars of the door…..he recited:

> To-morrow, and to-morrow, and to-morrow,
> Creeps in this petty pace from day to day,
> To the last syllable of recorded time;
> And all our yesterdays have lighted fools
> The way to dusty death. Out, out, brief candle!
> Life's but a walking shadow, a poor player,
> That struts and frets his hour upon the stage,
> And then is heard no more. It is a tale
> Told by an idiot, full of sound and fury,
> Signifying nothing.

Printed in the United States
By Bookmasters